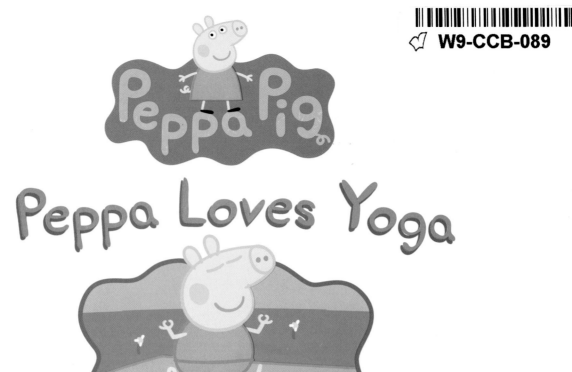

Peppa Pig

Peppa Loves Yoga

Adapted by Lauren Holowaty

Published by arrangement with Entertainment One and Ladybird Books, A Penguin Company.
PEPPA PIG and all related trademarks and characters TM & © 2003 Astley Baker Davies Ltd and/or Ent. One UK Ltd.
Peppa Pig created by Mark Baker and Neville Astley. All rights reserved. Used with Permission. HASBRO and all related logos and trademarks ™ and © 2021 Hasbro.

All rights reserved. Published by Scholastic Inc., *Publishers since 1920.* SCHOLASTIC and associated logos are trademarks and/or registered trademarks of Scholastic Inc.

ISBN 978-1-338-70145-6

10 9 8 7 6 5 4 3 2 1
Printed in the U.S.A.

21 22 23 24 25
40

First printing 2021

www.peppapig.com

SCHOLASTIC INC.

Licensed by

It's been a very busy morning at play group. Peppa and her friends have played instruments, dressed up in fancy clothes, and made the messiest of crafts.

"Now we are going to say hello to a visitor," Madame Gazelle says.

"Ooh," gasp the children. They wonder who the visitor is!

Briiiing!
Briiiing!

The visitor is at the door.
The children can't wait.
They start to cheer.

The visitor is Miss Rabbit!
The children jump up and
down excitedly.

"Namaste," says Miss Rabbit, putting her hands together and bowing slowly. "That is how we say 'hello' before yoga."

"What's yoga?" Danny Dog asks while waving his arms.

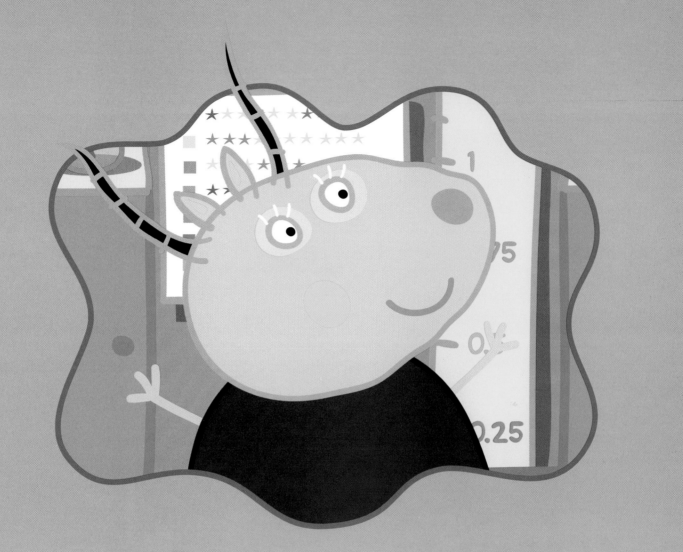

"Yoga is a way of relaxing," Madame Gazelle explains. "It's a bit like having a rest. And if you're feeling stressed, relaxing with yoga is a great way to calm down."

Peppa and her friends stop jumping.
"Namaste," they repeat, and slowly bow toward Miss Rabbit.

How to Pronounce Namaste:
NAH-meh-stay

Madame Gazelle is right. The children feel a little bit calmer. Then they follow Miss Rabbit outside.

Everyone sits on a mat outside.
"Now, touch your fingers and
thumbs together, and close your
eyes," Miss Rabbit says.
The children do.

Everyone breathes slowly through their noses to the count of three.

"One . . . two . . . three," says Miss Rabbit.

"*Phwwww*," breathe the children.

"Next, we will do tree pose," says Miss Rabbit. "Stand on one leg, and be as still as a tree. . . ." Everyone copies Miss Rabbit.

"Put your leg forward and bend into warrior pose," says Miss Rabbit. "I think this one is like being a surfer."

Everyone steps forward.
They like being surfers!

"You'll like this next one, Danny," says Miss Rabbit, putting her hands on the floor and lifting her tail into the air. "It's called the downward dog."

Then, Miss Rabbit stretches
up like a snake.
"And this one is called cobra
pose," she explains.

Finally, Miss Rabbit lowers her voice and whispers, "Now we must rest. Lie down on your backs while I count very slowly. One . . . two . . . three . . ."

It's time for the children's parents to pick them up.

"We've been doing some yoga," Madame Gazelle explains.
  "It looks very relaxing," says Daddy Pig.

"Yoga *is* relaxing," says Madame Gazelle. "I think we should do it every day!"
  Everyone loves yoga!

Try a Yoga Exercise, Just Like Peppa!

It was wonderful that Miss Rabbit came to visit Peppa and her friends at play group. But you can do yoga everywhere. Here are some tips to take yoga on the go and get a bit of relaxation.

❀ Take a big, deep breath in through your nose. Count to three. Then breathe out with your mouth.

❀ Stand up tall. Bring your arms to both sides. Move them upward, stretching out, over your head until they meet. Then release your arms.

❀ Close your eyes and count to three.

❀ Try Tree Pose or Yoga Pose.

❀ Use the cards in the back of this book to try new yoga poses.